JONATHAN CROW, DETECTIVE

by

Mary Adrian

Illustrated by Marie C. Nichols

Jonathan Crow knew more about the strange ways of animals than any other crow in the woodland. He was noted for his wisdom. His younger brother, Timothy, was caught spying and Jonathan saved him from being pecked to death. One mystery after another was solved by Jonathan and all the animals in trouble looked to him for help. Here are lots of fascinating nature stories, scientifically factual.

* * *

Dewey Decimal Classification: Fic

About the Author:

MARY ADRIAN wrote nature stories for many magazines, as well as a nature column for the Boston *Post* and a feature each month for *House Beautiful,* before she began to write books. She grew up on Long Island and went to New York University. In addition to her fiction and non-fiction books on nature, she has written a series of mystery stories for young people, one of which is *The Tugboat Mystery.* Her nature fiction always has a mystery in it. She is married and lives in Oregon.

About the Illustrator:

MARIE NICHOLS began to paint portraits of her children's pets, which started her in an art career. Friends commissioned her to paint portraits of their pets, so she became an animal portrait painter. She was born in Brooklyn, and now lives in Massachusetts. She studied art in Boston, but after two years married and settled down to raising a family. During World War II, she began again, this time with animals. Ten years and several hundred portraits later she turned to illustrating.

Jonathan Crow, Detective

Jonathan Crow,

Detective

By MARY ADRIAN

ILLUSTRATED BY
MARIE C. NICHOLS

1963 FIRST CADMUS EDITION
THIS SPECIAL EDITION IS PUBLISHED BY ARRANGEMENT WITH
THE PUBLISHERS OF THE REGULAR EDITION
HASTINGS HOUSE, PUBLISHERS INC.
BY
E. M. HALE AND COMPANY
EAU CLAIRE, WISCONSIN

Library of Congress Catalog Card Number: 58-11202

This edition lithographed in USA by Wetzel Bros., Inc., Milwaukee 2, Wisconsin

Contents

Foreword

Explanation: these stories of woodland creatures are based on scientific facts which are easier and more interesting to point out in action than to state coldly as true. Hence, because this book is intended for young children, I have put this information in story form. Also, I have taken the liberty of making up conversation between the birds and animals which, of course, could not take place. However, to anyone at home in the woods, it is obvious that there is some very definite sort of communication between the living things. I want my young readers to realize that this conversation is only an approximation of what this communication might be.

Mary Adrian

Jonathan Crow, Detective

The Trial of Timothy Crow

TIMOTHY was a young Crow. His feathers were black except one tail feather that was edged in silver. No one knew why Timothy's plumage was like this. It was something very rare in the crow kingdom.

Timothy loved to clean his silver feather. He loved to do something else, too, for he was a curious crow. He liked to spy on his fellow creatures and often he would follow them to their secret dens. He would also spend a lot of time flying about the woodlands, investigating strange tree hollows and exploring new places.

One day Timothy's curiosity got him into trouble—a lot of trouble that almost cost him his life.

13

He was sitting on the top of an oak tree whose branches stretched far and wide. It was a perfect lookout. He could see the fields of wheat spreading out like a sea of gold, and in the distance many trees crowded together like those in a forest.

Suddenly, a black speck appeared in the sky. Timothy was all attention, for he was certain it was his leader, Nicodemus, on one of his secret missions into the woodlands. But as the black speck came closer, Timothy found that it was not Nicodemus after all. It was one of his brothers, Jonathan Crow. He was an old crow, who knew more about the strange ways of animals than any other crow in the woodland. He was noted for his wisdom.

With a mighty sweep of his wings, Jonathan landed on the same branch that Timothy was using for a lookout.

"I am surprised to find you here," he said to Timothy. "I thought you would probably be spying on a sleeping owl."

"I have more important things to do," answered Timothy. "I am waiting for Nicodemus. He's been acting very strangely lately. Every

14

afternoon he disappears into the woodlands, and no one knows why he goes there, or what he does. I am sure it must be something secret, so I am going to follow him and find out what it is."

"I wouldn't if I were you," advised Jonathan. "Nicodemus might not like it. He's our leader. Why, every time we raid a cornfield, he gives the warning signal several seconds before the sentinel crows see the farmer coming with his gun! So if you are wise you will not spy on our leader. If he wishes to go on secret journeys that is his affair, not yours."

Timothy did not answer. He knew that Jonathan was right, but he also knew that he *must* find out the reason for Nicodemus' secret missions!

And so Timothy waited until later in the day, when his leader flew by the oak tree. Then, as silently as a shadow, he followed him into the woodlands. He was careful to stay far enough away so as not to attract attention. And when his leader swooped down and landed near the bank of a stream, Timothy lighted on a sycamore tree nearby.

Without so much as moving a feather, he

watched his leader scurry under a bush. Loose dirt began to fly in every direction, and in a little while Timothy saw that Nicodemus had unearthed a number of white pebbles and clam shells. It was his treasure chest. But among the articles was something else, something bright and shiny that glistened in the sunlight.

Nicodemus lifted the object with his beak, held it for several seconds, then put it down and looked at it from all sides.

After that he flew to the edge of the stream and searched along the bank until he found another clam shell. Adding this to his collection, he covered the articles with dirt, flapped his wings, and disappeared above the treetops.

Immediately, Timothy left the sycamore tree to investigate the shiny object in Nicodemus' treasure chest. He uncovered the dirt, looked among the clam shells and pebbles until he came across the shiny article. It was a silver coin.

Timothy picked it up. After examining the coin, he put it back with the other treasures. Then he shoved some of the loose dirt over everything and departed to tell his brother, Jonathan, of his discovery.

17

Sometime later, after Timothy had gone, Nicodemus returned to the stream with a piece of broken china that he had found near a house. It was not so choice as the silver coin, but he wanted to add it to his collection.

No sooner had he alighted at his hiding place than he gave a cry of alarm. Someone had uncovered his treasures, and that was not all. His coin was gone!

"A thief has been here," he cawed in a loud voice. "A thief has taken my coin!"

Then, suddenly, Nicodemus became very quiet, for not far from his treasures he saw a black feather edged in silver. He recognized the feather instantly. It was Timothy's feather—a feather he had just shed, for it was the end of the nesting season when birds begin to molt.

Nicodemus placed a pebble on the feather so that it would not blow away and so that he would have evidence to show who the thief was. With a broad sweep of wings, he then flew back to his home, a bulky nest in the top of a pine tree.

Right away he called for all the crows to come to a meeting.

Now, Timothy had just finished telling Jona-

18

than the reason for Nicodemus' secret journeys. And so he became alarmed when he heard his leader shout out about the coin. Had someone told Nicodemus that he, Timothy, had discovered his treasure chest? If so, who had told him?

All this Timothy was thinking as he flew to the pine tree where the crows had begun to gather. But when he faced Nicodemus, he could hardly believe his ears, for his leader said, "Timothy Crow, you are a thief. You stole my coin."

"I didn't steal your coin," cried Timothy. "Why, I wouldn't think of taking something that belonged to you!"

"Tell me this then," snapped Nicodemus. "Where is your silver feather?"

Timothy turned his head as far as he could and stared at his tail. "I guess I must have shed my silver feather. You see, I have just begun to molt and . . ."

"I know all about that," interrupted Nicodemus. "But I will tell you where your silver feather is. You left it near my treasure chest at the stream. You were spying on me, and I found the evidence. It's your feather, which I left

19

there for every crow to see. But before we hold a trial, you will give me back my coin."

"I didn't take your coin," answered Timothy. "Won't you believe me?"

"How can I believe you when you left your silver feather there?" replied Nicodemus. "You and the rest of the flock had better come with me and see the evidence."

In silence, Timothy followed his leader and the others to the crystal stream. When he saw his silver feather lying close to the white pebbles and clam shells, he did not know what to say. Certainly here was evidence that he was the one who had taken the coin. But really, all he had done was look at it, and then bury it with the other treasures.

Jonathan also stared at the evidence with a heavy heart, for he was afraid the crows would convict his brother, and he was fond of Timothy, even though his curiosity had gotten him into trouble. Then, too, he had witnessed several crow trials in his days. Whenever one of the flock broke a law, a trial was held, and if the offender was found guilty, he was pecked to death.

And so Jonathan felt that he should defend

Timothy because he did not believe that he was the thief. He joined the other crows, who had examined the evidence and were gathered in a nearby maple tree, waiting for the trial to begin.

"Timothy Crow, are you or are you not guilty?" said Nicodemus.

"I am not guilty," pleaded Timothy.

"But you spied on me, did you not?" asked Nicodemus.

"Yes," answered Timothy in a low voice.

"Well, then, you took my coin," replied Nicodemus. "And if you do not confess to this robbery, you will be punished."

"But I didn't take your coin," cried Timothy. "Honest I didn't."

"The evidence speaks for itself," answered Nicodemus. "No one else was here but you."

The other crows said nothing. Sitting there with their wings wrapped about them, they looked like judges in black robes. Timothy could almost tell what they were thinking. He tried to stop trembling, for the memory of the other crow trials he had seen was very vivid. The crowds had swooped upon the thief and killed him. Was this going to happen to him?

Just then Jonathan spoke up. "Please, Nicodemus, may I look once more at the silver feather. I do not believe that Timothy is guilty."

"You don't!" cried Nicodemus, so surprised that he shook his feathers furiously. But he respected Jonathan, especially because of his great wisdom.

"I am sure Timothy is innocent," continued Jonathan. "So if you will give me five minutes, I think that I shall be able to tell you who the thief is."

"All right, five minutes, but no longer," said Nicodemus. "This trial must come to an end."

"Thank you, Nicodemus." And Jonathan started back to the treasure chest—more curious to see an article that had puzzled him than the silver feather.

As he alighted on the ground, he gave a loud cry of alarm. A Pack Rat was there with one of Nicodemus's clam shells in his mouth.

He started to run, but Jonathan had already given the crow alarm signal, and his fellows were flying in from all around. In an instant, the crows encircled the Pack Rat, ready to strike him with their sharp beaks.

"What are you doing with my clam shell?" shrieked Nicodemus.

"I ... I ... was just making a trade," stammered the Pack Rat. "You see, I collect shiny things, and when I saw you looking at your coin this afternoon ..."

"The coin!" cried all the crows, coming closer to the Pack Rat, who kept backing away in terror.

"Quiet!" ordered Jonathan. "I will handle this. What did you do with the coin?" he asked the Pack Rat.

The animal shook with fright. "I ... I ... left something for the coin," he said in a weak voice. "You see, I'm not a thief. I'm a trader. I always leave something in return for what I take. That's why I left a toadstool. Didn't you see it?"

"Yes, I saw the toadstool when we were looking at the evidence a few moments ago," answered Jonathan. "It was under one of the clam shells. I couldn't figure out what it was doing among Nicodemus' treasures, so that's why I came back to look at it again."

"Jonathan, you are a master detective," said Nicodemus. "I never would have have suspected the Pack Rat. However, I do not wish to trade with him. I want my coin back."

"Yes, of course," said the Pack Rat. "I will get it for you right away."

The flock of crows followed the Pack Rat to his den, a large mound of sticks, pine cones, leaves, and rubbish. With loud cawing cries, they waited while he went inside and reappeared with the silver coin.

Then Nicodemus fondled his precious possession and flew back to his other treasures near the stream to bury them in another hiding place.

Timothy turned to Jonathan. "Isn't there something I can do to thank you?"

"Yes, there is," replied Jonathan. "Just remember that spying on others sometimes gets woodland folk into a lot of trouble."

"I'll remember that," answered Timothy. "And I'll never forget what you did for me. Wherever I go, I shall tell everyone that you are the master detective of the woodland."

The Witch of the Woods

A CHIPMUNK was hunting for acorns. He made a lot of noise for a tiny creature as he scurried through a bed of oak leaves. Except for the stripes on his back, his rusty brown fur matched the colors of his surroundings, and his sharp eyes searched for a nut the way a gull looks for a clam.

But alas, the Chipmunk was not able to find even one acorn, and since winter was coming, he had to have a supply of acorns or other nuts in his den.

Disappointed, he sat down under the oak tree. He rubbed one little paw over his face, then the other, and wondered where he should look next.

Presently a Blue Jay alighted on a stone wall nearby. He was a handsome bird with a gray breast, blue feathers, and a black ring around his neck.

"Have you found any nuts?" he asked the Chipmunk.

"No," replied the tiny creature. "I don't know what has happened to the harvest this year. It's very poor."

The Blue Jay agreed and then said, "I know where there are some hickory nuts."

"You do!" cried the Chipmunk. Then he regarded the Blue Jay with suspicion, for he knew he loved to tease. "Ah, you're just trying to get me excited. There are no hickory nuts around here."

"Yes, there are!" answered the Blue Jay. "There are a lot of hickory nuts on the ground at the edge of the North Woods, not far from a small tree with yellow flowers. I wouldn't advise you to go there, though, because . . ."

"Because why?"

"The Witch of the Woods is there," replied the Blue Jay.

"Now I know you're fooling," cried the Chip-

26

munk, spinning around and turning a somer-
sault in the leaves. "Why, whoever heard of a
witch in the woods! Only birds and animals
and insects live there."

"Go and see for yourself," said the Blue Jay.
"I heard about the Witch of the Woods from
the beavers, and they heard about her from the
bullfrog."

"Well, I still don't believe you," replied the
Chipmunk. And with a twitch of his perky tail
he started on his journey to the North Woods,
which was quite a distance away.

He walked through the meadow and then
climbed up onto a stone fence. It was a crooked
fence with large and small rocks piled up close
together. But the Chipmunk was sure of foot.
He scurried over the rocks until he reached the
end of the fence. Then he jumped to an old log,
paused to get his breath, and continued along
a winding path.

Finally, he came to the edge of the North
Woods. There, just as the Blue Jay had said,
stood the small tree with yellow flowers. Not far
away was a bed of withered leaves that had fallen
from a hickory tree.

27

The Chipmunk moved quickly as he hurried to the bed of leaves. He did not have to look long for nuts, since there were plenty of them scattered about. He ate some. Then, just as he was about to stuff one in his mouth to carry back to his den, he heard a popping noise. Snap! Snap! Snap!—like shots from a gun.

Instantly the Chipmunk dropped the hickory nut. His tail stood up straight, his ears perked up like a jackrabbit's.

One minute, two minutes, three minutes passed. The popping noise occurred again. Snap! Snap! Snap! And before the Chipmunk realized it, something struck him behind the ear.

This was too much for the Chipmunk. Like the unwinding spring of a watch, he leaped through the air and ran along a narrow path, crying in a terrified voice, "The Witch of the Woods! The Witch of the Woods!"

He did not stop running either until the North Woods were far behind him. With breath coming quickly, he stopped near the trunk of a tree to rest.

"What's wrong?" asked his cousin, the Gray Squirrel from a branch above. "You look as if something terrible has happened."

"It's the Witch of the Woods!" answered the Chipmunk, still trying to get his breath. "I've never been so frightened in all my life."

"Tell me about her," said the Gray Squirrel, becoming so interested that he ran down the tree trunk.

"She is at the edge of the North Woods, near a tree with yellow flowers," explained the Chipmunk. "I was just there, eating some hickory nuts. There are a lot of them on the ground."

"Hickory nuts!" cried the Gray Squirrel, waving his bushy tail. "I shall go to the North Woods right away."

"Oh, but you mustn't! Terrible things happen there. I didn't believe the Blue Jay when he told me about the Witch of the Woods. I do now, though."

"Did you see her?" asked the Gray Squirrel.

"No. That's just it," replied the Chipmunk. "It's all very mysterious. Something pops along the ground—like shots from a gun. And something hit me in back of the ear. I thought it was the hunter who had fired his gun, but I couldn't see him. So it must be the Witch of the Woods."

29

"No, it's the hunter," said the Gray Squirrel. "And I know how to dodge him. I'll run to the other side of a tree trunk. I've done it many times before, and it always works. Besides, I wouldn't give up a hickory-nut feast even if there *was* a witch there. She wouldn't scare me." And the Gray Squirrel hurried to the North Woods.

When he reached the hickory nuts, he ate several, thinking all the while that the Chipmunk must have been imagining things. Why, there was nothing here to frighten anyone—no hunter in sight, and certainly no Witch of the Woods!

The Gray Squirrel ate some more hickory nuts. Then, just as he was about to carry one back to the tree where he lived, he heard the popping noise. Snap! Snap! Snap!

The Gray Squirrel dropped the nut and like a flash of lightning ran up the hickory tree. He flattened himself against the trunk and with beating heart waited for another shot.

Nothing happened. Only a flock of geese, winging their way South, passed over the treetops. They were followed by a group of Monarch Butterflies, who had started on their long trip South. Their orange-and-black wings looked

30

like tiny parachutes as they flitted through the air.

The Gray Squirrel did not watch the butterflies go by, for he was still clinging to the tree trunk. After a while he peeked around the other side. There was no trace of a hunter, and he could not understand that because those shots certainly sounded as if they came from a gun.

The Gray Squirrel waited a little longer and then slowly went down the tree trunk headfirst. Cautiously he walked through the bed of leaves, hunting for a hickory nut. No sooner had he found one than the same loud popping noise came again. Snap! Snap! Snap!

The Gray Squirrel looked this way and that way when something suddenly hit him behind the ear.

Like an arrow he zoomed past the hickory tree, past the tree with yellow flowers, and on in the direction of home.

"How did you make out?" asked the Chipmunk when the Gray Squirrel reached the stone fence.

"You were right," answered the Gray Squirrel. "There *is* a Witch of the Woods. I am not

31

going back to the North Woods again, even though I love hickory nuts. But it's a pity that we can't store them away for the winter when there are so many."

"Why don't we outsmart the Witch of the Woods?" suggested the Chipmunk. "Now, if we could get those hickory nuts without her seeing us, everything would be all right."

"That's an idea," said the Gray Squirrel. "How shall we go about it?"

"Let's ask Jonathan Crow," answered the Chipmunk. "I heard he's a master detective. He'll tell us what to do. He'll even tell us who the Witch of the Woods is."

"Fine!" said the Gray Squirrel. "We will talk to Jonathan Crow."

They found him perched on a log. He listened carefully to everything they had to say, and his head bobbed up and down when they spoke of the popping noise that sounded like shots from a gun.

"This is a very interesting case," he said. "And it may not be hard to solve. I will fly to the North Woods and report to you what I have found. I'll be back in a little while."

But Jonathan Crow was gone quite a long time, and the Gray Squirrel and the Chipmunk wondered what was keeping him.

"Maybe he's afraid of the Witch of the Woods and doesn't want to tell us," said the Gray Squirrel.

"No, my guess is that he is checking on all the facts," replied the Chipmunk. "That's why he is a good detective."

Sure enough, the Chipmunk was right. While he was gone, Jonathan Crow had thoroughly investigated the popping noise that sounded like shots from a gun.

Now he was ready to report to the Chipmunk and the Gray Squirrel what he had found.

"If you will come with me to the North Woods," he said, "I might be able to show you who the Witch of the Woods is."

"Are you sure it's all right to go there?" asked the Chipmunk. "What we want to do is to outsmart the Witch of the Woods and get those hickory nuts without her seeing us. Of course, we would like to know who she is."

"Come with me, then," said Jonathan Crow. "And perhaps you will learn all about her."

So the three of them started for the North Woods. Jonathan Crow flew from tree to tree, while the Chipmunk and the Gray Squirrel ran along the ground.

But once they reached the hickory nut tree, the Chipmunk and the Gray Squirrel wanted to leave right away.

"Don't be frightened," said Jonathan Crow. "The Witch of the Woods won't hurt you, and when you hear the shots, don't run away."

The Chipmunk and the Gray Squirrel did not answer, for they were really scared. Even the hickory nuts at their feet did not tempt them. They looked around when suddenly without warning, came the popping noise. Snap! Snap! Snap!

With a leap and a bound, the Chipmunk and the Gray Squirrel started to run.

"Don't go!" cried Jonathan. "You'll find out something very amazing if you'll look at the tree with the yellow blossoms."

The Chipmunk and the Gray Squirrel came to a dead stop. They stared cautiously at the tree with the yellow flowers. Then they held very still, as still as statues. The tree was shooting out

35

little black objects into the air. Each one made a noise like a tiny shot from a gun.

"Those black things are the tree's seeds," explained Jonathan.

"Her seeds!" The Chipmunk was so surprised that he jerked his tail up straight.

"Yes," answered Jonathan. "When you told me about hearing shots from a gun, I investigated and found out that it was coming from this tree. So I went and asked the beavers if they could tell me more about the tree with the yellow flowers. They explained that she is the Witch Hazel Tree, and that she is the only tree in these woods to bloom and bear fruit in the autumn. When she throws out her seeds, they make such a frightening noise that many woodland creatures call her the Witch of the Woods."

The Chipmunk twitched his whiskers with relief. "Now that I know about the Witch Hazel Tree, I'm not afraid of the Witch of the Woods any more."

"Neither am I," answered the Gray Squirrel.

And together the two woodland creatures hurried to the bed of hickory nuts to store away food for the winter.

The Magic Spider

IT was a busy time in the rose garden. Ants were milking "honey cows," those tiny green bugs called aphis that cling to the stems of rosebushes. They stroked them with their feelers until the bugs gave them drops of sweet juice, which was the sap they had sucked from the rosebush and turned into honeydew.

"This is the best honeydew I have ever tasted," said one ant. She was adventurous, always ready to explore new hunting grounds.

"It certainly is good juice," said another ant. She was greedy, always wanting more than the others. "I'm going to the next rosebush and milk some more honey cows."

"Don't go there!" cried the Wise Ant, who

knew a lot about the creatures in the woodland. "That's the bush where the Magic Spider lives. See her web."

"Yes, I see it," answered the Greedy Ant. "But I'm not afraid of the Magic Spider."

"I saw an ant killed by the Magic Spider," continued the Wise Ant. "She wasn't afraid either, but you know what happened when she fell into the web. The Spider came from nowhere, just like magic. And that was the end of the ant."

"How terrible!" said the other ants as they listened to the Wise Ant's story. "We won't go near that rosebush. Honeydew is not worth that much to us."

"It is to me," said the Greedy Ant. "I'm going to climb that rosebush."

"So am I," added the Adventurous Ant. "I'll stay away from the Spider's web, and then nothing will happen to me."

It was not long before both ants were climbing up the mysterious rosebush. And the higher they climbed, the more they waved their feelers, for there were so many honey cows that they did not know which ones to milk first.

The Wise Ant watched from the other bush. "Don't go any farther!" she cried. "The Magic Spider will come after you, if you do."

The Greedy Ant paid no attention to the warning. Ahead of her, not far from the web, was a cluster of honey cows, which would soon be all hers. But she was so eager to get to them that she pushed the Adventurous Ant aside.

"What's your hurry!" cried the Adventurous Ant. "There are plenty of honey cows for both of us."

The Greedy Ant did not answer. She pushed some more, not realizing that she was getting closer to the web. The next thing she knew she slipped and fell into the trap.

"Oh, dear!" she cried, as she struggled to free herself from the sticky threads that bound her like the ropes of a net.

The Adventurous Ant wanted to help, but she was afraid that she might also fall into the dreaded trap. So all she did was to run this way and that way, until suddenly she scurried down the bush in terror. The Magic Spider had appeared from nowhere—a great yellow creature with eight legs and eight eyes.

With the speed of an electric flash, the Spider ran across the silver threads of her trap. But instead of making a dash for the Greedy Ant, she stopped and shook the web for all she was worth. She had a reason for doing this. She wanted to make sure that another creature, who had accidentally stepped into her web, would not get away.

It was a Praying Mantis. She was a big bug, lots bigger than the Spider, and many tiny woodland creatures were afraid of her. But not the Spider. She wanted to capture the Praying Mantis.

"You don't frighten me," she said. "I've heard about the hooks on your front legs that are like sharp knives. They won't hurt me, though, because I'm going to throw sticky threads around you so that you won't be able to move."

"Go ahead and try it," answered the Praying Mantis.

With the skill of an expert, the Spider threw out a strand of silk to lasso her huge prize. Instantly, the Praying Mantis raised her forelegs with their sharp hooklike knives. The Spider backed away, waited a moment, and then rushed

40

toward her prisoner again. But once more she was driven back.

Now, the Greedy Ant, still struggling to free herself from the web, was afraid that the Spider would give up trying to capture the Praying Mantis. And if that were the case, she would become the Spider's victim instead. The Greedy Ant dreaded to think what would happen to her.

But the Spider was not one to give up easily. More than ever she wanted to kill the Praying Mantis. And even though a sudden gust of wind shook the web, she kept trying to lasso the huge insect. She threw out another line of silk and ran toward her prisoner. This time she came too close. The forelegs of the Praying Mantis snapped upon her with the spring of a steel trap.

Frantically, the Spider tried to get away, but the sharp blades tightened around her. Then the wind began to blow with such force that several strands of the web broke. The Praying Mantis, with the Spider still clutched in her forelegs, fell to the ground.

Someone else tumbled out of the web, too— the Greedy Ant. She scrambled to her feet and ran down the garden path, not stopping until she

came to a flat boulder where ants from her colony had gathered.

"Are you hurt?" they cried.

"No. I'm all right. But I'll never go back to that rosebush again. It was terrible. If the Praying Mantis had not gotten the Spider, the Spider would have killed me instead."

"I know," agreed the Adventurous Ant. "I wanted to help you, but that Spider—I'll never forget her. She was magic. Why, she came from nowhere, and someone must have told her that you fell into the web because she appeared so quickly! I wonder who it was."

"Jonathan Crow can tell us," spoke up the Wise Ant. "He's a detective and can tell us everything that goes on in the woodland."

"Yes, I know all about the Magic Spider," said Jonathan Crow, after the ants had questioned him. "Her real name is the Shamrock Spider, and if we go back to her web, I will show you something that will amaze you. However, I will need a volunteer to crawl up the rosebush and follow my instructions."

"Oooh! I never want to go near that bush again," cried the Greedy Ant. "I know there are a lot of honey cows on it, but they don't mean that much to me."

"No one will hurt you," said Jonathan Crow. "The Praying Mantis by this time has killed the Spider."

"I'm still afraid," answered the Greedy Ant. "I don't want to take any more chances."

Jonathan Crow looked at the other ants, but no one volunteered. "Well, I guess we won't talk about the Magic Spider any more. It's a shame, though, because if one of you were to go to her broken web, you would see something you would never forget."

"I'll go!" cried the Adventurous Ant.

Soon she was climbing up the mysterious rose-bush, while Jonathan Crow began giving instructions from a tree nearby.

"Crawl around the broken web and tell me what you see," he cawed.

Cautiously the Adventurous Ant moved around the broken web. She took her time, for, although Jonathan had said no one would hurt her, she wanted to be sure that another Magic Spider was not lurking close by.

But all the Adventurous Ant could see were

44

loose strands of the web, tossing back and forth with the wind.

"There is nothing here," she cried, nervously waving her feelers.

"Yes, there is," answered Jonathan Crow. "Look at the silk line running from the center of the web. Follow it and see where it goes."

Very cautiously the Adventurous Ant crawled forward on the rosebush. Then, suddenly, she came to a dead stop.

"Don't be frightened," called Jonathan Crow. "What you are looking at is the tent of leaves where the Magic Spider was hiding. See the opening she made when she rushed out?"

"Yes! I see it!" cried the Adventurous Ant. "And that silk line—why, it runs from her web to her hide-out in the tent of leaves."

"That silk line is her telephone wire," explained Jonathan Crow. "The Spider is smart. She tries to make you think she's magic. She hides in her tent of leaves, and then as soon as someone touches her web, out she comes!"

"My goodness!" cried the Adventurous Ant. "Now, when I see a web and no spider around, I'll watch out."

The other ants had no peace until they, too, investigated the Spider's telephone signal and her tent of leaves. Even the Greedy Ant crawled up the mysterious rosebush and saw what an intricate system she had escaped from.

The Vanishing Rabbit

THERE was much excitement in the woodlands where a stream, edged with willow trees, ran through a hollow. In one of the trees sat a strange bird. Except for some gray spots, his feathers were as white as the snow on the ground.

A flock of crows, circling around the hollow, had discovered the strange bird. In their eagerness to find out who he was, they flew close to look at him. Then they darted away, since they had never seen a bird like him before, and they were frightened by what they did not know. Also he sat so still, without blinking an eye or moving a feather. Where had he come from, and why was he as white as the snow?

Finally, Timothy Crow, curious young Timothy, swooped down and landed on the top of the tree. He did not stay long, for a loud warning cry filled the woodland.

"Danger! Danger!" shrieked Jonathan Crow from a stone wall where he could see all that was going on.

The crows quickly gathered around him. They were full of questions, but Jonathan hushed them by turning to Timothy and saying, "Don't you know better than to go near that bird! He's the Snowy Owl."

"Well, then, if he's an owl, I can tease him," cried Timothy. "You know how much I love to chase owls because of what they do to us."

Jonathan knew only too well what the Great Horned Owl did to crows at night. He would fly silently through the woodlands and swoop down upon a sleeping crow and kill him. Because of this, the crows spent a lot of time looking for the Great Horned Owl in the daytime when he does not hunt. Whenever they found him sleeping in a tree, they would wake him up and bother him. Then they would give him a merry chase, and the owl, not being able to see well in the sunlight, would fly blindly from tree to tree until he was exhausted.

So all the crows felt the same as Timothy. No matter what kind of owl the strange bird was, they wanted to get even with him.

"But the Snowy Owl is different from other owls," cried Jonathan. "I'm an old crow and I've seen only one Snowy Owl in these woodlands. This bird came down from the North, and hunted in the daytime, not at night. Now if you are wise you'll let this owl alone."

Timothy drew his feathers closely about him. "I'm glad you warned me, Jonathan. I'd better tell everyone in the woodland about this owl, especially that he kills crows in the daytime. But I wish there was a way we could get even with him."

"I know a trick we can play on the owl," said Jonathan Crow.

"You do?" cried the others. "Tell us what the trick is, Jonathan."

"Sh! Not so loud. I don't want the Snowy Owl to hear us talking. We'd better go to my maple tree."

Soon a small flock of crows were gathered

around Jonathan, waiting to hear about his plan. They sat on the branches of the trees, with heads cocked and feathers wrapped around them.

"There's a Rabbit who lives in the briar patch," said Jonathon. "I saw her taking a sun bath a little while ago. Now all we have to do is to go back to the hollow, sit on the stone wall, and say in a loud voice that we saw a Rabbit near the briar patch. And if my guess is right the Snowy Owl will hunt that Rabbit right away."

"But what about the Rabbit? Suppose she gets killed?" a young crow inquired.

"She won't," Jonathan assured him. "At least if I'm right, she won't."

"Then what is the trick we're going to play on the Snowy Owl?" asked Timothy.

"You'll see," replied Jonathan.

"I want to know now," wailed Timothy. "Right now."

"Don't be so impatient," said Jonathan. "It's half the fun not to know what the trick is."

"Oh, well, all right," answered Timothy.

But he was so anxious to fool the Snowy Owl that he was the first one to arrive at the stone wall. With the others he cawed as loud as he could, telling the whereabouts of the Rabbit, and he bobbed up and down each time he called it out.

Presently the Snowy Owl heard him and could not resist hunting for food. He stretched out his great wings and, like a flying ghost, glided through the air. He did not make any noise either, for like all owls the tips of his feathers were covered with tiny mufflers of soft down.

Jonathan, Timothy, and the other crows immediately followed the Snowy Owl, and when he alighted on a tree near the briar patch, they started to chant about the Rabbit again. This time Jonathan led the chorus.

"The Rabbit has left the briar patch," he cried. "She's in the clearing. Her tracks are in the snow."

The Snowy Owl turned his head this way and that way to look for the Rabbit, but all he saw were footprints—a long trail of them that dotted the blanket of snow.

"I don't see the Rabbit," whispered Timothy to Jonathan. "Is that what you made up to fool the Snowy Owl?"

"No. The Rabbit is somewhere around, as

sure as I am here," answered Jonathan. He said it in a loud voice so that the Owl would hear him.

The other crows were as puzzled as Timothy. They strutted up and down where the snow was not heavy, and left behind them tracks that criss-crossed many times. But all the while they kept watching the Snowy Owl, for they did not trust him. If there was no Rabbit here and that was the trick that Jonathan was playing on the Owl, the Owl might decide to strike out and grab one of them instead.

That is exactly what the Snowy Owl had in mind, but just then Jonathan Crow cried out in an excited voice, "Look! The Rabbit must have been sunning herself alongside this rock. You can see where she was sitting."

Timothy flew over to the rock. The tracks were there, sure enough, but where was the Rabbit? Surely, she could not have vanished that quickly, and if she had, where did she go? It was a mystery to Timothy, curious Timothy, who was always eager to find out about things.

But it was more of a mystery to the Snowy Owl, who was getting so hungry that he wanted to find the Rabbit right away. He circled around the rock and then covered the clearing from beginning to end, his eyes never for a moment leaving the Rabbit's trail in the snow.

Finally, Jonathan Crow could not remain silent any longer. He began to squawk like a hen, and then he whined like a dog.

The Snowy Owl became so confused that he did not know which way to turn—a rabbit, a hen, and a dog, and he could not see any of them. This was more than he could bear—the crows must be up to some tricks! Well, he would show them!

He made a dash for Timothy, but Jonathan quickly gave the warning signal—a signal that made Timothy, as well as the other crows, fly away as fast as the wind was blowing.

"Come to my maple tree," Jonathan called to them after he made sure they had lost the Snowy Owl. "I've got a lot to tell you."

"You certainly have," answered Timothy. "I didn't know that you could squawk like a hen and whine like a dog."

"Yes, I used to be quite good at it when I was younger," replied Jonathan, smoothing out his feathers. "Of course, I will admit that not all

53

crows can imitate the way I can. It's one of my pet tricks, and I guess I fooled the Snowy Owl, didn't I?"

"You surely did," answered Timothy. "But that Rabbit—I'll bet she wasn't there at all."

"That's where you're wrong, Timothy. You just didn't see her. She's not brown like other rabbits. Her coat of fur is as white as the snow."

"What kind of rabbit is she?" asked Timothy, eager to hear more about her.

"She's the Snowshoe Rabbit," answered Jonathan. "Sometimes she is called the Varying Hare, and she changes her coat twice a year. In the spring her fur is brownish-gray like the brush around her. In the fall her fur begins to change and when the cold weather comes, it is pure white, except for the black tips of her ears. She can run fast, too, because her feet are covered with a heavy coat of fur. They're like snow-shoes."

"So that's how she got her name—the Snow-shoe Rabbit!" concluded Timothy. Then he added, "I'll bet the Snowy Owl is still looking for that Rabbit."

54

"If he isn't, I've given him something to think about," said Jonathan Crow. "The Snowy Owl might have white feathers, but he's not the only one who can hide in the snow."

The Riddle
of the Black Snake

TOADS hopped down to the pool to lay their eggs. Butterflies left their cocoons and dried their wings before making their first flight. And birds flitted here and there, bursting with song as they built their nests.

Jonathan Crow sat in his maple tree and watched the happy woodland creatures. Then he did something he could not resist doing—he played his favorite game of "Waking the Sleepers."

Other crows were playing it, too—a group of young ones, and, although Jonathan was twenty years old, they were glad to have him join them.

Like dark clouds moving across the sky, they

57

flew over the woodlands until they came to a pasture where some cows were taking a nap.

Darting from a great height, the crows landed on the backs of the cows and cawed in their ears at the top of their lungs. The cows opened their big eyes, startled.

Then the crows left the pasture to look for more sleepers. Jonathan Crow found a rabbit dozing in the shade of the briar patch. He swooped down and pecked her on the head.

Instantly, the Rabbit woke up, and before Jonathan Crow could tease her any more, she ran into a hole in the ground.

She stayed there for some time until she heard a commotion in the orchard. Jonathan heard it, too, and immediately went to investigate. He found several birds flying around the apple tree where Jenny Wren had made her home in a deserted woodpecker hole. Outside it a Black Snake had suddenly appeared and had frightened the little bird before it glided off again.

"Don't worry, Jenny Wren," cried the orchard birds. "We'll find out where the Black Snake has gone."

"And I'll peck at him with my sharp beak so

that he will never want to hunt here again."

The Kingbird was a small bird with a white breast and a patch of orange on the top of his head. Many feathered folk called him the policeman of the air because he chased away birds much larger than himself, and he would attack a hawk, if necessary. Now he was ready to attack the Black Snake, who not only liked to eat toads and mice, but baby birds as well.

But where had the Black Snake gone? It was a mystery to Jenny Wren's friends, since they had searched the apple tree from top to bottom and they could not find him anywhere.

"Are you sure you saw the Black Snake?" the Kingbird asked Jenny Wren.

"Of course I'm sure," she answered. "He climbed up this tree and looked inside my doorway, and if I hadn't been here, he would have eaten one of my babies. Now I must go and get food for them, but I'm afraid to leave the nest because I don't know where the Black Snake is hiding."

"I know just how you feel," comforted Maggie Robin. "Cock Robin is guarding my nest. Otherwise, I wouldn't be in your tree. But I won't have any peace until we know where the Black Snake is hiding."

"Neither will I," answered the Catbird, who had her nest in the bushes nearby.

Just then the Blue Jay flew into the orchard. "I found the Black Snake," he said, sitting on the top of Jenny Wren's tree. "He's in the meadow not far from the wooden fence."

"In the meadow!" cried Maggie Robin. "How did he get there so quickly?"

"He crawls along the ground as fast as lightning," answered the Blue Jay. He turned to the Kingbird. "Aren't you going to chase the Black Snake out of the meadow?"

"I certainly am," replied the Kingbird. And in a twinkle he darted above the orchard trees and into a wide-open space of green grass and wild flowers.

Maggie Robin and the others followed. Even Jonathan Crow, whose keen eyes always told him a lot, went with them. And while the Kingbird searched one end of the meadow, he inspected the other. He circled around, hoping to catch a glimpse of the Black Snake gliding through the grass.

But the grass was quiet in the meadow, as still as the leaves on the trees. So Jonathan Crow flew over to the fence where the Blue Jay was sitting and sat down beside him.

"I am convinced that you didn't see the Black Snake at all," he said.

"I did, too," cried the Blue Jay. "I saw the Black Snake in this meadow. And if he isn't here now, he's gone somewhere else."

Jonathan Crow regarded the Blue Jay thoughtfully. Deciding he was telling the truth, the old crow began to hunt some more for the Black Snake. He even searched the woodlands and looked in every nook and corner and behind every rock and log that he came to.

At sunset, however, Jonathan Crow had not found the Black Snake. Feeling discouraged, he sat in his favorite maple tree and watched the birds flying about the orchard getting food for their young. They seemed uneasy, though, and hurried back to their nests every few minutes, while the Kingbird still looked for the Black Snake.

Presently the Blue Jay flew into the orchard.

"Have you found the Black Snake?" he asked the Kingbird.

"No," replied the policeman of the air. "And I don't believe you saw him in the meadow. You made that up to frighten the little birds."

The Blue Jay ruffled up his feathers in anger. "Why is it no one will believe me?" he screamed at the top of his lungs. "I guess when it's too late and the Black Snake has eaten one of your babies, you'll say the Blue Jay was right. He did see the Black Snake."

The Kingbird did not answer. Only Jenny Wren believed the Blue Jay, for hadn't she seen the Black Snake herself? Why, he might have returned to the orchard and was hiding where no one could see him!

In a zigzag fashion Jenny Wren flitted over to the maple tree to talk over the seriousness of the matter with Jonathan Crow.

"Let me give it a little thought, Jenny Wren," said the old crow. "In the morning I will do some more investigating."

True to his promise, Jonathan was up very early. The first place he visited was the Great-Crested Flycatcher's nest in the hollow of an elm tree. She was not at home, but what Jonathan saw in her nest made him get very excited. He walked around the foot of the tree and looked every which way until the Flycatcher returned.

"What are you up to, Jonathan?" she asked, knowing his reputation for being a good detective. "Are you trying to solve another mystery?"

"Indeed I am. The Black Snake is hiding in these woodlands, and I think you can tell me where to find him."

For several minutes the Great-Crested Flycatcher chatted with Jonathan Crow.

"Thank you, Flycatcher. I shall go there right away." And he flew to a rock in a flower garden. Not far from it, lying on the ground, was the Black Snake. He was taking a sun bath.

Jonathan quickly flew to the top of a tree. In a loud cawing voice, he said, "I found the Black Snake. I found the Black Snake."

In a matter of seconds the birds came flying from every direction, and the first one to arrive was the Blue Jay.

"I was right, wasn't I? I did see the Black Snake."

Jonathan Crow nodded and then watched the Kingbird fearlessly swoop down and peck at the Black Snake. The creature moved like an arrow shooting through the garden. But the Kingbird was not finished. While the birds circled around and cried out in excited voices, he struck the snake again with his sharp beak.

In a flash the long black creature disappeared under a stone wall on the next farm.

Pleased with himself, the Kingbird flew to a tree where Jonathan Crow and the other birds soon gathered around him.

"You did some fine work," Jonathan told the Kingbird. "The Black Snake won't be in a hurry to come out of hiding now."

"I should say he won't," added Jenny Wren. "And I am glad he left the orchard."

"So am I," said Maggie Robin. "Tell us how you tracked down the Black Snake, Jonathan."

"Yes, tell us," cried the others.

Jonathan Crow flicked his tail feathers with importance. "I guess I know quite a bit about a snake," he said. "He gets rid of his old skin in the spring, just as we shed our feathers in the summer. So I decided that if I could find the Black Snake's old skin, I might be able to tell where he was hiding. And guess where I found it?"

"Where?" asked the birds in a loud chorus.

"In the Great-Crested Flycatcher's nest."

"I can't believe it!" cried Jenny Wren.

"Jonathan Crow is right," answered the Flycatcher, who had joined the group. "I always use the old skin of a snake to line my nest."

"How horrible!" cried Maggie Robin.

"I don't see anything horrible about it," protested the Flycatcher. "I think the old skin of the Black Snake is beautiful. It's almost pure white, and I am glad I used it for my nest because it helped Jonathan Crow to find where the Black Snake was hiding."

"It certainly did," answered Jonathan Crow. "If you hadn't told me where you found the Black Snake's old skin, I would still be looking for him."

The Flycatcher began to clean her feathers. Then she darted back to her home in the elm tree.

"There is no one like the Great-Crested Flycatcher," said Jonathan Crow. "And no one knows why she lines her nest with the old skin of a snake. It's a mystery of the woodland."

66

The Missing Nuts

A GRAY SQUIRREL climbed up the hickory tree. He walked out on a long limb and waved his bushy tail. This helped to balance him. He watched the leaves twirl through the air and fall to the ground. And he looked at the buds on the branches of the tree which held the fresh leaves for next spring.

Then all at once the Gray Squirrel began to chatter to himself. He saw two hickory nuts hanging from one of the branches. Now he would be able to store away his favorite food. He would bury the nuts in the ground so that when winter came, his keen scent would tell him where he had hid these nuts. Then all he would have to do was to dig them up.

The Gray Squirrel leaped from one branch to the other until he came to the hickory nuts. He picked up one and, holding it in his mouth, started down the tree trunk headfirst, as if he were walking along the ground.

On the other side of the tree a Nuthatch, a white-breasted bird with bluish-gray feathers, came down the trunk as the squirrel had—not backwards, but headfirst.

The two met at the foot of the tree—the Gray Squirrel, waving his bushy tail, the Nuthatch chirping a song.

But the Gray Squirrel paid no attention to the little bird. He hurried over to a flat rock nearby, and, after leaving the hickory nut there, he went back for the other nut. This one he also left on the rock, and then he looked for a place to bury his two prizes.

At last he found just the spot, under a crooked apple tree. Waving his bushy tail, he dashed back to the rock, then he opened his eyes wide, for his nuts were not there.

"My nuts!" he cried. "Who took my nuts?"

He looked at the Nuthatch, who was hopping through a bed of leaves. "You took my nuts. Give me back my nuts."

The Nuthatch turned around, and stared at the Gray Squirrel. "I haven't got your nuts."

"Yes, you have," scolded the Gray Squirrel. "I left two hickory nuts on this rock, and they're gone."

"I didn't take them," answered the Nuthatch. "Besides, I didn't see any nuts there, so you must have imagined it." And he flew away, high above the trees in the orchard.

The Gray Squirrel flicked his tail in anger, and then walked around the rock several times to see whether the nuts had fallen off.

"Are you looking for something?" called the Blue Jay from the hickory tree.

"Indeed I am," cried the Gray Squirrel. And he climbed up the tree as fast as he could make his legs move. "Give me back my nuts," he shouted.

"Nuts! What are you talking about?" answered the Blue Jay.

"You know perfectly well what I mean," snapped the Gray Squirrel. "I left two hickory nuts on that rock, and you took them."

"Now I wouldn't do a thing like that," replied the Blue Jay, hopping farther out on the branch and cocking his head to one side.

69

"Oh, yes, you would!" cried the Gray Squirrel. "I've watched you hide acorns and chestnuts in hollow trees and in the grass and under leaves. So give me back my hickory nuts."

"I don't believe you found any hickory nuts at all," said the Blue Jay. "You just imagined it."

"No, I didn't," scolded the Gray Squirrel. And he ran out on the branch after the Blue Jay.

But the handsome bird was too quick for him. He spread out his wings and darted through the air just as the Gray Squirrel came face to face with his cousin, the Red Squirrel.

Now, the Red Squirrel was smaller than the Gray Squirrel. He liked to tease as much as the Blue Jay did. But more than that he liked to fight, and for this reason the Gray Squirrel never played with him. In fact, he was a little afraid of his cousin.

"Er, did you take my nuts?" he asked.

"If I did, I certainly wouldn't tell you," answered the Red Squirrel, waving his skimpy tail. "But the Blue Jay is right. You just imagined you found some nuts. Why, if there were hickory nuts left on this tree, I would be the first to see them—not you!"

"Is that so!" snapped the Gray Squirrel.

"Yes. That's so!" the Red Squirrel snapped back. And he came so close to his cousin that the Gray Squirrel could feel his breath on his cheek.

Quickly the Gray Squirrel jumped to another branch and then to another tree. The Red Squirrel ran after him, dashing along limbs and up and down tree trunks until he finally caught up with his cousin. Then he nipped one of his hind legs.

This was too much for the Gray Squirrel. He jumped from the tree and sailed through the air until he hit the ground. He landed on his feet, unharmed, for his bushy tail had saved him.

In a fury of speed, the Gray Squirrel rushed off into the woodlands. But later, in the afternoon, he came back and sat on the flat rock near the hickory tree.

Suddenly he heard a bird chirping almost on top of him. He looked around, but he could not see a bird anywhere.

"That's strange," he chattered to himself. "A bird singing and no bird!"

Never before had the Gray Squirrel heard

anything like this, and he was sure that a bird was singing—just as sure as he was that someone had taken his prize hickory nuts. But who was the thief? Who had taken them?

Finally, the Gray Squirrel went to look for Jonathan Crow. The crow would be able to tell him who had taken his hickory nuts. He searched for him in the orchard, in the meadow, at the edge of the North Woods, and at last found him sitting in his favorite maple tree.

The Gray Squirrel watched Jonathan preen his feathers.

"I may be an old crow," said Jonathan, "but I still remember to clean my feathers."

"You remember lots of things," praised the Gray Squirrel. "And you find out about things, too."

Then the Gray Squirrel spoke of his hickory nuts, and said that he suspected either the Nuthatch, the Blue Jay, or the Red Squirrel of taking them.

Jonathan Crow listened and, looking very wise, said, "I'll tell you one thing—the Nuthatch did not take your hickory nuts. He likes soft-shelled nuts, such as acorns and chestnuts. You see, his bill is too weak to break open the shells of hard nuts like the hickory nut or the walnut."

"But what about the Blue Jay?" asked the Gray Squirrel. "He hides nuts."

"Yes. He loves chestnuts and acorns. But he loves to tease, too. And I am sure he would not hesitate to take your hickory nuts, no more than the Red Squirrel would. So I will watch these two rascals, and see if I can't track down your prize nuts. Now is there anything else that happened at the rock where you left your nuts?"

"No," answered the Gray Squirrel. "Come to think of it, though, I heard a bird singing, but I didn't see any bird. It was the strangest thing I have ever come across."

"I don't think it was strange at all," answered Jonathan Crow. "You stay here, and I'll come back and report to you in a little while. I am sure by that time you will have your nuts back."

With that Jonathan Crow flew through the woodlands and alighted on the ground near the hickory tree. He walked around the flat rock, listening all the while very carefully, until he heard a bird singing. Then he flew to a stone wall and hid in some bushes close by.

74

It was not long before he saw all he wanted to see. With a sweep of his saw-toothed wings, he flew back to the maple tree where he found the Gray Squirrel waiting for him.

"Did you find any nuts?" asked the Gray Squirrel.

"Yes. Come with me, and I will show you who took your nuts."

But the Gray Squirrel wanted to know right away. "Was it the Blue Jay or the Red Squirrel?" he asked.

"Come with me and you will see," was all Jonathan would say. And he led the Gray Squirrel to the bushes near the stone wall.

"I don't see my nuts," wailed the Gray Squirrel.

"You will in a minute," answered Jonathan Crow as he scratched around in the dirt. "They are here under this log. The Chipmunk put them there. He sometimes does that with nuts before he stores them in his burrow. That's his home, dug in the ground under the stone wall."

"But how did you know that the Chipmunk took my nuts?" asked the Gray Squirrel. "I didn't suspect him."

75

"No, I guess you didn't. You see, the Chipmunk carried away your nuts in the pockets of his cheeks. I've seen him carry as many as twelve hazel nuts in one trip. Of course, then his cheeks were puffed out almost three times the size of his head."

"The Chipmunk is quite remarkable," agreed the Gray Squirrel. "But I still don't know how you found out that he took my nuts."

"I will tell you," explained Jonathan Crow. "When you told me that you had heard a bird singing, and you couldn't see a bird, I knew that the Chipmunk must be around, and that he must have taken your nuts. Few woodland folk know that he sings like a bird. I wouldn't have known if he hadn't fooled me once."

"Yes, the Chipmunk certainly fooled me," answered the Gray Squirrel.

He picked up one of the hickory nuts and, holding it in his mouth, ran to a place to bury it in the ground. But first he made sure that the only one watching him was Jonathan Crow.

The Strange Signal

THE RACCOON lay stretched out on a branch of the oak tree in the meadow. He had slept most of the day, as all raccoons do, and soon he would fish for his dinner in the stream nearby.

But right now he was watching a young Rabbit nibble at some clover not far from the oak tree. He had seen the Rabbit before, for it was her custom to come out from the briar patch and go to the bed of clover. Sometimes her mother came with her.

This afternoon, however, the young Rabbit was alone.

Suddenly, and without warning, a large bird began circling over the meadow. It was the

Hawk, who was greatly feared by the little wood-land folk.

Now, the Raccoon saw the Hawk flying over-head. He wanted to warn the Rabbit. But before he could do so, the Rabbit took to her heels and disappeared into a hole in the ground, just as the Hawk swooped down, ready to grab her in his claws.

This made the Hawk so angry that he cried at the top of his lungs. Then with a broad sweep of his wings, he flew upward and high into the sky.

The Raccoon blinked his eyes in wonderment. He had witnessed many strange things taking place in the woodland, but nothing had ever happened as mysterious as this. He could see no one around who had warned the Rabbit. And he knew she could not have seen the Hawk, because her back had been turned to him. Yet she had hopped away before the huge bird was able to catch her.

As the Raccoon sat there, thinking about the incident, he saw Jonathan Crow fly into the meadow.

"You're just the one I want to talk to," he

called, moving over so that Jonathan could perch alongside him.

Then the Raccoon told the old crow how the Rabbit had escaped from the Hawk, and how he was certain that no one had warned her.

"It's a mystery to me how she got away, Jonathan," he added. "But I'm sure you'll know. You're the master detective of the woodland. You've solved many mysteries for us woodland creatures."

Jonathan puffed up his feathers. He loved to receive praise, especially for his detective work.

"I'll tell you what I'll do, Raccoon," he said. "You go and fish for your dinner. When you come back, I might be able to tell you how the Rabbit was able to dodge the Hawk. Right now it is a bit confusing to me, and I want to do a little investigating."

"Fine, Jonathan. I'll go down to the stream for my dinner. I'm getting hungry anyway."

The Raccoon uncurled his handsome tail that was wrapped around him. Humping up his back, he crawled along the branch until he came to the tree trunk. Then, digging his claws into the bark, he made his way headfirst down to the ground. After that he shuffled through the underbrush in the direction of the stream.

Suddenly a twig snapped. The Raccoon was all attention. He sniffed the air and looked around for enemies. But all he could hear was the rustle of the wind in the trees. So, cautiously, he continued on his way until the sound of rippling water came to his ears. This made him hurry to the stream. He waded into the shallow water and felt along the muddy bottom with his paws for crayfish.

Finally, he found a crayfish under a stone. He swished it around in the water, for that is what raccoons do. They wash their food before eating it. Then the Raccoon climbed up the bank of the stream and started to eat his dinner.

No sooner had he finished it than he shuffled through the underbrush again, anxious to find out if Jonathan Crow had solved the mystery.

He found his friend sitting on a higher branch of the oak tree.

"Come on up," called Jonathan. "And you had better hurry if you want to see what's going to happen."

The Raccoon climbed up the tree as fast as

he could make his legs move. When he reached Jonathan's perch, he was so excited that he had a time settling himself comfortably.

"Tell me quickly, Jonathan. What did you find out about the Rabbit? How did she escape from the Hawk?"

"You'll soon find out," answered the old crow. "The Hawk is due here any minute. He always comes back to a hunting ground until he makes his catch."

The Raccoon looked up into the aerial highway. There was no bird in sight. Only a dragonfly darted about, flying in a huge circle. The Raccoon watched the insect until it zoomed off into space, and then he fixed his attention on the Rabbit. She was eating clover again, her nose buried in the white flowers.

"Goodness," said the Raccoon. "The Rabbit certainly isn't afraid of the Hawk coming back."

"The Hawk is here now," whispered Jonathan. "See? He's flying overhead."

The Raccoon held his breath. Then he twitched his whiskers nervously, for the Hawk had swooped down and was flying low over the meadow. The Rabbit was still eating clover.

The Raccoon could not stand the suspense a minute longer. "Jonathan, we had better warn the Rabbit," he said. "I'm sure she doesn't know the Hawk is here."

Before Jonathan could answer, the Rabbit went into action. She jumped into the hole a fraction of a second before the Hawk made his final plunge.

This was too much for the Raccoon.

"I don't understand it, Jonathan. How did the Rabbit know the Hawk was here?"

"That's easy to explain," replied the old crow, wrapping his feathers about him as he always did when he was about to answer an important question. "If you will look over there at the foot of the maple tree, you will see someone sitting alongside the brush."

The Raccoon blinked his eyes and then stared as hard as he could. "I don't see anyone," he said.

"Mother Rabbit is there," replied Jonathan Crow. "I'll admit she's hard to see. I had a time finding her myself because her fur blends in with the color of the brush."

The Raccoon stared some more. "I see her now," he cried. "She's thumping on the ground

83

with her hind feet. Why is she doing that?"

"That's the answer to the mystery," explained Jonathan Crow. "The mother Rabbit is telling the young Rabbit that it is safe to come out of the hole. She wants her baby to know that the Hawk is gone. You see, she was the one who warned the young Rabbit. She saw the Hawk circling overhead and gave the signal by thumping with her hind feet, which is the way rabbits talk. They signal with their feet, and the sound carries very far along the ground."

"Thank you, Jonathan, for solving the mystery," said the Raccoon. "Now I think I'll go and fish for some more dinner."

With that the Raccoon climbed down the tree. Before shuffling off to the stream he stopped to tell the young Rabbit that Jonathan Crow had told him her secret.

"But we won't tell anyone," he said, "because we don't want the Hawk to find out."

The Phantom of the Forest

REMY was a young deer who lived in the forest. He loved the whispering pines, the tall maple and oak trees, and the dogwood and laurel thickets. He loved the pond with its floating lily pads, which he and his mother feasted upon at daybreak and at sundown.

But since the day when the hunter had fired his gun and killed Remy's mother, the young deer had been alone with only the Bullfrog as his friend.

Now Remy came to the lily pond to share a secret with the Bullfrog. He was growing his first antlers and he wanted to show them to his friend.

"My, my!" croaked the Bullfrog. "I can hardly believe that you are growing your first antlers.

Last year you were just a young fawn who came with his mother to the lily pond to eat the lily pads. Now you are growing up. And soon you will be a buck, a handsome buck with antlers."

Remy's eyes glowed with happiness as he listened to the Bullfrog's words of praise. But no sooner had he nibbled at a lily pad than he heard a noise in the underbrush. Instantly Remy glided into the water and hid among the lily pads.

"Why are you hiding?" asked the Bullfrog.

"Sh!" said Remy. "I heard someone, and I want to find out who it is."

One minute, two minutes passed. A twig cracked. And Remy held his breath, for at the water's edge he saw two little deer—Danny and Jenny. They were fawns and were still wearing their baby coats of rich brown fur with white dots.

Remy watched them, fascinated. He had always wanted to play with other deer, and these two looked very friendly.

"What are you waiting for?" croaked the Bullfrog. Don't tell me you are afraid of two little deer."

"No. I'm not afraid. Only . . ."

"Only what?" asked the Bullfrog.

"I don't know them, and maybe they don't want to play with me."

"Why, Remy! Of course they want to play with you. But they've run off into the forest now. The next time you see them, though, be sure and ask them."

It was not until many weeks later that Remy saw the two deer again. They were playing tag in an open space, and, as he watched them from a hazel thicket, he noticed that they were wearing their winter coats of dusky gray. Around and around in a circle Danny chased Jenny until she stopped to get her breath.

Remy wanted more than ever to play with Danny and Jenny, but once again he was afraid to ask them. So he stayed in hiding, yet he could not help listening to what they were saying.

"Danny, do you think we will ever see the Phantom of the Forest? Mother has seen him. Grandfather Buck has seen him. I think everyone has seen him except us."

"If we search the woodlands long enough, I am sure we will find the Phantom," replied Danny.

"I hope we will find him soon," answered Jenny. "Grandfather Buck says that the Phantom is the most beautiful creature he has ever seen in this forest. And Grandfather Buck has lived here a long time."

Danny blinked his eyes in silence, for he longed as much as Jenny to see this beautiful creature of the forest—the Phantom. Waving his tail from side to side, he said, "Let's look in the laurel thicket. Maybe we will find him there."

As the white tails of Danny and Jenny disappeared in the heavy brush, Remy glided out of his hiding place. His eyes were filled with excitement, for he, too, wanted to see the Phantom of the Forest. So he hurried to the lily pond to ask about him from his friend the Bullfrog.

But when Remy reached the lily pond, he found that the Bullfrog had gone to sleep for the winter—a sleep that would not end until the following spring.

Disappointed, Remy looked about him. Only several lily pads floated on the water, and they were a pale yellow. The willow trees at the end of the pond had shed most of their leaves. During the warm summer days Blackbirds had

88

alighted on the branches of the willow trees. Now only a Snowbird could be seen, for the Blackbirds had left for the South.

Remy looked up at the Snowbird. "Have you been here long?" he asked.

"Not very long," chirped the Snowbird. "I have just flown from the North. Why do you ask?"

"There is a very beautiful creature in this forest," replied Remy. "I have never seen him. But everyone calls him the Phantom. And I thought that perhaps you might know where I could find him."

The Snowbird thought a moment. "I am afraid I can't help you. But on my way into the woodlands I flew past some Beavers at work in a pond. Perhaps they have seen the Phantom of the Forest."

"Thank you. I shall go there right away."

With a graceful leap Remy disappeared into the thick woods. His legs moved like magic as he glided over thickets and around large trees. Presently he reached the pond. It was much larger than the lily pond. At one end was the beaver dam, where water flowed over it in long crystals. At the edge of the pond stood the beaver house, a dome-shaped structure of mud and sticks.

Remy went over to a group of beavers who were slapping wet mud against the outside walls of their house. "Please, can you tell me where I might find the Phantom of the Forest?"

An old beaver looked up from his work. "We're much too busy to answer questions to-day. Winter will soon be here and we must plaster our house so that the walls will freeze and keep our enemies out. Sorry we can't be of some help to you. You might ask Jonathan Crow, though. He knows everything that goes on in these woodlands."

"Thank you. I'll do that."

And Remy began to look for Jonathan Crow. But he could not find him anywhere, and since it was almost night, he decided to go to his sleeping place. It was a cave, hidden by trees which grew out of two larger rocks. There, Remy slept peacefully until daybreak when he awoke and looked out of the cave. The first thing he saw was a blanket of snow on the ground and on the trees.

90

Remy pawed at the snow until he uncovered some withered leaves. After he had eaten them, he went along one of his old trails. He leaped over logs and jumped over laurel bushes until he came to an open space. Then he stood very still and sniffed the wind. It told him something very important—a hunter was in the woodlands.

Cautiously Remy continued along his trail until he came to another open space. Then he held very still again. This time it was because he saw Danny and Jenny standing near a tree. They were looking for food, and with them was Grandfather Buck, the biggest deer that Remy had ever seen. His antlers spread out like branches of a tree.

Remy watched the two little deer with the same longing—to go over and play with them. Suddenly he began to sniff the wind again. He threw back his head and took a deep breath. Then he became rigid, like a statue, for the wind told him that the hunter was close by.

The next thing Remy knew he saw him standing a short distance away from Grandfather Buck and the two little deer. But before the hunter could raise his gun and fire, Remy snorted.

91

Instantly Grandfather Buck and Danny and Jenny disappeared into the woods.

The hunter followed their tracks in the snow, but they soon became so jumbled that he could not tell where the deer had gone.

"I don't understand it," he said aloud. "Who could have warned them? There was no other deer around." And the hunter walked on, very much puzzled at what had happened.

Meanwhile Remy glided through the woodland. He was still looking for Jonathan Crow, for he wanted to find the Phantom of the Forest more than ever.

Finally, just when Remy had about given up, he saw Jonathan in the apple orchard.

Now, Remy had never visited the orchard before, so he hesitated leaping over the snow-covered ground to the fruit trees.

"It's all right. No one will see you," called Jonathan Crow.

Still Remy hesitated. "The hunter is around," he said. "I saw him a little while ago."

"So did I," answered Jonathan Crow. "But he'll never see you because you're the Phantom of the Forest."

92

"You must be mistaken," cried Remy. "I couldn't be the Phantom of the Forest. Why, the beavers told me to ask you about him! And Grandfather Buck says he's the most beautiful creature he has ever seen."

"But *you* are the Phantom of the Forest," insited Jonathan Crow, looking very wise. "You're an albino deer with a coat of fur as white as the snow. That's why the hunter didn't see you and you were able to warn Grandfather Buck. I heard all about it. And Danny and Jenny want to play with you."

"They do!" cried Remy, his brown eyes sparkling with joy. "They really want to play with me?"

"They certainly do," said Jonathan Crow. "You see, it is very rare for a deer to be born with a white coat. I have lived in these woodlands a long time, and you are the first white deer I have seen. That's why we call you the Phantom of the Forest."

Remy waved his tail from side to side. Then with graceful leaps he hurried into the woodlands to look for Danny and Jenny.

The Cry of the Hawk

IT was spring in the orchard. Bees darted about the apple blossoms, eager to drink the sweet nectar. Birds alighted on the branches, their throats swelling with joy as they warbled their songs.

Suddenly a whistling scream filled the air. It was the cry of the Hawk, and it told the small birds that he was hunting for food.

Instantly Jenny Wren flew to her nest, a hole in a crooked apple tree. Chippy, the Sparrow, dropped a caterpillar she was eating and hurried to her home. And Maggie Robin flew to her nest on a low branch of a peach tree, where she was joined by her mate, Cock Robin.

After that it was quiet in the orchard, with only the bees humming around the blossoms. Then one bird, another, and still another started to leave her nest. Each one looked about the orchard to see where the Hawk might be hiding. He was nowhere in sight. So the birds, feeling all danger was past, darted about the fruit trees looking for food until—the whistling scream filled the air again.

In a twinkling the orchard was deserted with every bird back on her nest.

Maggie Robin was so frightened that she could not stop her feathers from trembling.

"It's all right," she heard someone say. "I'll take care of you."

She looked around. On a branch near her nest sat the Kingbird. He was the policeman of the air—fearless, ready to attack the Hawk, who was much larger than he.

"Just stay where you are," said the Kingbird to Maggie Robin. "I'll find the Hawk, and I'll chase him so far away from this orchard that he won't want to hunt here again."

Maggie Robin sat back on her nest and fluffed out her feathers to keep her eggs warm. She felt relieved that the Kingbird was going to guard the orchard.

But the Kingbird was not having much success finding the Hawk. Every tree he came to, there was no sign of reddish-brown feathers hiding among the blossoms.

Finally, the Kingbird reached the last tree in the orchard. He flew from branch to branch and was about to look inside Jenny Wren's house when she greeted him in the doorway.

"Don't tell me you're hunting for the Hawk in my house!" she cried. "He's much too big to come in here. He might be hiding in a tree hollow, though. There's one in a dead apple tree at the other end of the orchard. Did you look there?"

Before the Kingbird could answer, the tiny Hummingbird zoomed up to him and said, "You are needed in the meadow. The Black Snake is out hunting, and I am afraid he'll find the Meadowlark's nest in the grass. Of course, I could stab the Black Snake with my sharp beak and scare him away, but I need your help. So come quickly!"

"Yes. Yes. I'll come right away," said the

Kingbird, so excited that his tail feathers bobbed up and down.

"But you can't go to the meadow!" cried Jenny Wren. "You're guarding the orchard, and the Hawk is still hiding here."

"That's right," answered the Kingbird. "I almost forgot about him. I can't go to the meadow."

"Yes, you can," called a voice from the next tree. It was Jonathan Crow, who had been sitting there all the time. "I'll attend to the Hawk," he said. "As a matter of fact, I know where he is hiding this very minute."

"You do!" cried the Kingbird, wondering whether to believe Jonathan or not.

"I certainly do," replied the old crow. "So you take care of the Black Snake, and I'll take care of the Hawk."

"All right," answered the Kingbird. "I'll leave you in charge of the orchard." And he and the Hummingbird departed for the meadow.

Jonathan Crow then flew to Jenny Wren's tree. He spread out his feathers to let the sun warm them.

"Aren't you going after the Hawk?" asked Jenny Wren.

"Er . . ." was all Jonathan said, for just then the whistling scream floated over the orchard again. This time it sounded so loud that Jenny Wren quickly backed inside her tree hole. She waited, feathers quivering, until finally she looked outside once more. Jonathan Crow was still taking a sun bath.

"Why don't you do something?" she demanded.

"There is nothing to worry about," replied Jonathan, flicking his handsome tail feathers.

"Nothing to worry about with the Hawk in the orchard!" cried Jenny Wren. "Why, I don't think you know where he is hiding at all."

Jonathan Crow did not answer. With a sweep of his wings, he flew low over the fruit trees and disappeared in some brush close by.

Jenny Wren did not see him after that until a short time later when he returned to her apple tree with the Blue Jay. The two birds sat on a branch outside her tree hole and chirped in low voices.

"I don't know why you want me to help you find the Hawk," the Blue Jay said to Jonathan

Crow. "You're a detective. So you should know where the Hawk is hiding."

"I do," answered Jonathan. Then he added. "Sh! I hear a cat crying."

The Blue Jay cocked his head and listened. At nesting time he always helped his mate guard their young, especially against cats.

"The cat must be after your family," said Jonathan. "Her cries sound as if they're coming from the tree where you have your nest."

This was all the Blue Jay needed to hear. He darted to the next tree, a hickory tree at the edge of the orchard. He looked on each branch for the cat. Then he looked at the high grass below. Then he held very still, for the cat started to meow again. This time her cries sounded very, very close.

"Oh, dear!" cried the Blue Jay's mate, who was sitting next to their nest. "If the cat comes up this tree, she'll surely see our nest, and she'll eat our babies. So do something to make her go away."

"But I can't see any cat," answered the Blue Jay. He was so excited that he began to scream at the top of his lungs.

101

Finally, Jonathan Crow came to calm the Blue Jay.

"I'm sorry I had to do this to you," he said. "It was the only way I could teach you a lesson. There is no cat around here. I asked the catbird to imitate the cry of a cat to frighten you."

"You certainly scared me," answered the Blue Jay. "Don't ever do it again."

"I won't," answered Jonathan Crow, "If you promise that you won't imitate the cry of the Hawk. You see, I saw you hiding behind some leaves on that apple tree. You were whistling like the Hawk."

The Blue Jay moved uneasily on the branch where he was sitting. "I only did it to tease Jenny Wren and the other birds," he said.

"You only did it to tease us!" shrieked Jenny Wren, popping out of her doorway where she had been listening to the Blue Jay and Jonathan Crow talking. Her feathers were fluffed up in anger. And even though she was only half the size of the Blue Jay, she tried to strike him with her beak.

The Blue Jay dodged just in time and darted off, flying high above the trees in the orchard.

102

Jenny Wren smoothed down her feathers and went back to her doorway. Before entering her tree hole, though, she said to Jonathan Crow, "Won't the Kingbird be surprised to hear that it was the Blue Jay who screamed like the Hawk?"

"No doubt he will," answered Jonathan Crow, bobbing his tail feathers. "And if I know the Blue Jay, he'll think twice before he teases again."

Mystery in the Pond

A MOTHER DUCK led her babies down to the pond for a swim and a meal.

"Watch out for turtles," she warned them. "Don't go too far from shore."

The ducklings, six of them, waded into the water, and, like tiny sailboats, drifted around near the shore.

"Now we will dive for something to eat," quacked Mother Duck.

The ducklings dived under water and stood on their heads with their tails and flat webbed feet sticking up in the air above them.

Tiny fish swam by them and tadpoles darted here and there, moving like streaks of lightning.

The ducklings reached out and snapped up some tadpoles in their broad beaks. Then they poked around in the mud in the shallow part of the pond and ate several snails. Mud got into their mouths, but the ducklings did not mind. They had strainers on the sides of their beaks, and all they had to do was to close them tight shut so that the mud and water would be sifted out.

After the ducklings had eaten enough, they swam on the still waters of the pond, leaving little ripples behind them. But soon the wind made bigger ripples appear on the pond, and the ducklings bounced back and forth as they sat on the water.

Suddenly their eyes opened wide and they looked at their mother in alarm. Loud quacking came from one end of the pond where the male ducks were swimming among the reeds and grass floating on the water.

"Stay here and hide among the water plants, and don't go away until I come back," Mother Duck told her ducklings. "I'm going to see what the trouble is." Jumping out of the water, she flapped her wings and flew in the direction of the noise.

The ducklings quickly took cover among the water plants. They could hear more quacking coming from the end of the pond, and they could see birds flying overhead.

Then Maggie Robin, Jenny Wren, and the Blue Jay swooped down and landed on a tree where they could watch what was going on.

Mother Duck circled around the end of the pond with the male ducks, whose green heads glistened in the sunlight and whose chatter could be heard far and wide.

"It was awful!" they kept saying. "Red Fox didn't give us any warning. He sneaked up on us and grabbed the finest and best duck that ever lived in this pond."

Mother Duck knew that it was her mate they were speaking of. He had become the victim of Red Fox! At this she quacked so loud that the other ducks flew around and tried to comfort her.

Presently they all went and sat on the water in the middle of the pond.

"Didn't any of you see Red Fox swimming about?" asked Mother Duck.

"No. That was just it," answered a young duck. "Red Fox came from nowhere. Now this pond is no longer a safe place for us to swim in. We'll have to find another pond or a lake."

"But I don't want to leave this pond," grumbled an old duck. "I think we should stay here and outsmart Red Fox. All we have to do is to watch out for danger, and as soon as we see something strange, warn the other ducks."

"How are we going to do that?" asked Mother Duck. "If Red Fox left no clues, we won't be able to tell if he is swimming in the pond when we can't see him."

"True, quite true," admitted the old duck. "But I know someone who will be able to help us. His name is Jonathan Crow, and I've heard he's a good detective. He'll trail Red Fox and tell us what tricks he is up to."

"Let's go and find Jonathan Crow right away," quacked the other ducks. And they swam in to shore.

Mother duck hurried back to her ducklings, who were still hiding among the water plants. She led them to one end of the pond where they climbed up the bank and rested on the ground. Never for a moment, though, did Mother Duck forget that Red Fox was at large. She waddled back and forth and looked into the high grass and the woodland beyond.

Finally, she heard a crow cawing at the other end of the pond. She guessed it must be Jonathan Crow, for the male ducks were quacking, not in alarm, but in friendly chatter. Mother Duck wanted to go and join them, but she felt it would not be wise since her ducklings might start to wander and that is what Red Fox would want. So she kept guard, watching over her brood, while the male ducks swam about the waters of the pond.

Night fell upon the woodlands. Only the murmur of the wind in the trees and the cry of an owl broke the stillness. At dawn, however, came Jonathan Crow's voice, ringing out loud and clear. He was sitting in a tree close by.

"Tell me if you see anything strange in the pond," he called to the ducks.

The ducks paddled through the water, looking here and there for something that was unfamiliar to them.

"All I see is a bunch of grass floating on the water," quacked one duck. "And I've seen that many times before."

109

"Do you see anything else?" cawed Jonathan Crow.

"Just a stick and some more grass," quacked the duck.

Jonathan said nothing more. He went and hid in the hollow of the tree with only his head peeking out. His two sharp eyes saw everything that was going on below.

The ducks began to chatter because they could not see Jonathan, and they wondered why he had suddenly left them. But since there was nothing to alarm them in the pond, they decided he must be trailing Red Fox.

After a while some more grass floated out on the pond and soon caught up with the ducks, who were peacefully sitting on the water. Then came another bunch of grass, moving in the same direction.

"Look out!" cawed Jonathan Crow at the top of his lungs. "Red Fox is behind you."

The ducks jumped from the water, and, on whistling wings, circled round and round the pond. All they could see in the water, however, was a bunch of grass. And then suddenly a head emerged from the grass. It was Red Fox swimming back to shore.

110

He climbed up the bank, shook the water from his fur, and then stole silently back into the woodlands.

The ducks quacked and quacked—so glad were they to see him go. Soon they landed on the shore near the tree where they had last seen Jonathan Crow. They waddled around the big trunk and quacked, "Where are you, Jonathan? Where are you?"

Jonathan peeked out of the hollow in the tree, and the next thing the ducks knew he was walking on the ground with them, as if he had been there all the time.

"I never would have guessed that Red Fox was that smart," said the old duck.

"Yes, he's smart," answered Jonathan Crow. "I watched him from the hollow of this tree. First, he sent out a bunch of grass on the pond to fool you. Then he picked up another bunch of grass. This he held in his mouth, while he began swimming right for you ducks. Of course, you couldn't see him because his head looked just like another bunch of grass and the rest of him was under water."

"So that's why we didn't see him the first

112

time," said the old duck. "At least we fooled him the second time, thanks to you, Jonathan. Why, if you hadn't warned us, Red Fox would have caught us! Now that we are on to his tricks, though, we'll never trust a bunch of grass again."

"I should say not," said Mother Duck.

"I should say not," repeated the ducklings. And off they went for a swim in the pond.

The Mysterious Blue Tail

PERKY THE SKUNK could catch more grass-hoppers than any skunk in the woodland. In fact, he was known as the Champion Grasshopper Catcher. Ever since he was old enough to get his own food, he had showed how well he could catch grasshoppers. And although he hunted a lot at night, he also visited Grasshopper Meadow in the daytime.

Right now he was so full from eating grass-hoppers that his stomach had puffed up like a balloon. It dragged along the ground as he walked through the meadow. However, this did not stop Perky from catching more grasshoppers. He waited for one to jump. Then he jumped, too, and quickly pounced upon it.

Finally, Perky walked back to the log where the hunting had been the best. He wanted to take a sun bath. Before he could climb up on the log, however, he stepped on something that made him draw away in alarm.

It was a bright blue tail, thin and spiny. It was attached to nothing. It had no head, no stomach, no legs. But, even so, it wiggled and squirmed on the ground!

Perky knew it was not a snake. He had seen several of them gliding through the grass in the meadow. This thing was different. It frightened him, so much so that he decided to look for other hunting grounds.

The next day, shortly after sundown, Perky went to a different meadow. To his dismay there were few grasshoppers there. So he walked down the road, hoping to find another meadow.

Presently he met Silver Stripe. He was a young skunk who liked to tease Perky whenever he had the chance.

"You don't look as if you caught many grass-hoppers today, Perky," he said. "I guess you're no longer the Champion Grasshopper Catcher."

116

"I am, too," snapped Perky. "I can catch more grasshoppers than you can."

"Prove it then," answered Silver Stripe. "We'll go to Grasshopper Meadow and see who is the best hunter."

Silver stripe started down the road. Then, realizing that Perky was not following him, he turned and said, "Aren't you coming?"

"Yes, I'm coming." Perky's voice did not sound very enthusiastic. He tagged behind Silver Stripe. When they reached Grasshopper Meadow, he decided to let the skunk hunt near the log. It was by far the best hunting place in the meadow. But Perky felt sure that Silver Stripe would not stay there very long, not after he saw the mysterious blue tail.

A short while later Perky was surprised to hear Silver Stripe announce that he had caught lots of grasshoppers.

"I've caught more than I can eat," he said. And he came over to see how Perky was getting along.

But Silver Stripe soon found that Perky's stomach did not bulge the way his did.

117

"I knew it!" cried the young skunk. "I'm the Champion Grasshopper Catcher now. I shall tell everyone in the woodland that I can catch more grasshoppers than Perky."

Perky stamped his feet in anger. "You only caught a lot of grasshoppers because I let you hunt near the log. I wouldn't have if something very mysterious hadn't frightened me away yesterday."

"What was that?" asked Silver Stripe.

"It was a blue tail without any head. And it wiggled and squirmed on the ground."

"You must have imagined you saw a tail," replied Silver Stripe, "because I didn't see one. And I'm glad I hunted near the log because I sure caught a lot of grasshoppers, more than you'll ever catch."

"You're not being fair," cried Perky. "If I had hunted near the log, my stomach would be much bigger than yours. Yesterday it dragged along the ground. Yours doesn't. So I am still the Champion Grasshopper Catcher."

"No, you're not," replied Silver Stripe. And he left the meadow, repeating over and over to

118

himself that he was the Champion Grasshopper Catcher.

Perky was so upset that he went to consult Jonathan Crow. He found him perched on a stone wall, looking at the field in front of him. Perky climbed up on the fence and sat down next to the old crow.

"Jonathan, you're the master detective of the woodland," he said. "So I've come to talk to you about something."

Perky then related how he had seen a mysterious blue tail near the log in Grasshopper Meadow, and how Silver Stripe had caught a lot of grasshoppers there in spite of the tail. In fact, Silver Stripe had said the tail wasn't there.

"Now Silver Stripe claims he is the Champion Grasshopper Catcher," finished Jonathan Crow.

"Exactly," answered Perky, glad that Jonathan understood. "But I wish I could find another strange tail near the log. I know it would scare Silver Stripe away."

"It certainly would," replied Jonathan. "The mysterious blue tail has frightened many wood-land creatures."

"Then you've seen one?"

Jonathan nodded.

"Tell me about it. What kind of tail is it? And why is it so mysterious? It has no body. Yet it wiggles and squirms." Perky was so anxious to hear what Jonathan had to say that he waved his plume-like tail back and forth.

"I would rather wait for a while before I tell you everything about the mysterious blue tail," said the old crow. "I just thought of something that will make Silver Stripe stay away from Grasshopper Meadow. But you must promise that you will follow my instructions, Perky. You may be scared, but nothing will hurt you. If you do as I say you can be the Champion Grasshopper Catcher."

"I promise to do everything you tell me to do," said Perky.

"All right. Bring Silver Stripe to Grasshopper Meadow tomorrow at sundown."

The next day at the appointed time Perky and Silver Stripe met Jonathan Crow.

"Let's go over to the log," said the old crow.

"Are Perky and I going to catch grasshoppers?" asked Silver Stripe.

"Don't ask questions," said Perky. "Just do as Jonathan says."

Perky led the way. He drew closer and closer to the log. But before he reached it, a strange little woodland creature ran along the log. She was coal black and brightly striped.

"Who is that?" asked Silver Stripe.

Perky did not answer. He looked at Jonathan Crow.

"Come and hide behind this bush with me," said the old crow.

Perky and Silver Stripe did as Jonathan suggested.

The small creature soon jumped down from the log. She scurried by the bush and then stopped a moment.

"Catch her, Perky," said Jonathan Crow.

In a flash Perky had the small creature in his paws. In another flash he let out a scream of terror. The creature was gone, and Perky held only a blue tail in his paw—a tail that moved back and forth with short, quick motions.

Instantly Perky dropped the squirming tail. He started to hurry away with Silver Stripe.

"Perky, don't go!" called Jonathan Crow.

121

"Remember what you promised."

Perky came to a sudden stop, but not Silver Stripe. He was so frightened at what he had seen that he left Grasshopper Meadow as quickly as possible.

"I guess Silver Stripe will never want to hunt grasshoppers in this meadow again," said Jonathan Crow.

"No, I'm sure of that," answered Perky. "But tell me, Jonathan, who was the small creature? And what about her tail? Why it snapped right off when I grabbed it!"

"That's what the Blue-Tailed Lizard does," replied Jonathan Crow. "When someone attacks her, she sheds her tail. I'll admit it's very frightening the way it wiggles and squirms. It gives the lizard time, though, to get away from her enemy. Then she grows a new tail."

"I suppose someone must have caught a Blue-tailed Lizard the other day when I saw a squirming tail."

"That's right," answered Jonathan. "You see, I was sure there were two Blue-Tailed Lizards in this meadow, for I've watched them run along

122

the log at sundown. For this reason I wanted you to catch one to frighten Silver Stripe away from your hunting grounds. Now that you know all about these lizards, you can catch all the grasshoppers you want."

"Yes, I'm still the Champion Grasshopper Catcher," answered Perky. "Thanks to you, Jonathan."

The old crow puffed up his feathers. Then he flew to his favorite maple tree and folded his plumage around him. With his keen eyes he stared into the meadow below, waiting to discover another woodland mystery.

BIBLIOGRAPHY

Allen, Arthur A., Ph.D.:
American Bird Biographies, Comstock Publishing Co., Ithaca, New York, 1934.

Anthony, H. E., Technical Editor:
Animals of North America, Garden City Publishing Co., Garden City, L. I., New York, 1937.

Devoe, Allen:
This Fascinating Animal World, McGraw-Hill Book Co., New York, 1951.
"Our Fine-Feathered Friend," *Nature Magazine,* October 1943.

Ditmars, Raymond L.:
The Reptiles of North America, Doubleday, Doran & Co., Garden City, L. I.. New York, 1944.

Fisher, G. Clyde, Editor:
Nature Encyclopedia, Halcyon House, New York, 1940.

Pearson, Gilbert T., Editor-in-Chief:
Birds of America, Garden City Publishing Co., Garden City, L. I., New York, 1936.

Rogers, Julia Ellen:
Trees Worth Knowing, Doubleday, Doran & Co., Garden City, L. I., New York, 1928.

Rutledge, Archibald:
"Dangerous Beauty," *Nature Magazine,* December 1938.

BIBLIOGRAPHY

Seton, Ernest Thompson:
Lives of Game Animals, Volumes I, II, III, IV, Doubleday, Doran & Co., Garden City, L. I., New York, 1925.
Wild Animals I Have Known, Charles Scribner's Sons, New York, 1903.

Swain, Ralph B., Ph.D.:
The Insect Guide, Doubleday & Co., New York, 1948.

Teale, Edwin Way:
Grassroot Jungles, Dodd, Mead & Co., New York, 1937.
The Junior Book of Insects, E. P. Dutton & Co., New York, 1953.

8